Notes from the Shadow City

Gary William Crawford

Bruce Boston

Introduction:
Michael R. Collings

Dark Regions Press

2012

Poems included in this collection, some in slightly different form, have appeared or are forthcoming in *Aphelion, Bête Noire, Cast Macabre, Cover of Darkness, Dreams and Nightmares, The Gothic Revue, The Horror Zine, Paper Crow,* and *Star*Line.*

The following appear here for the first time: "The Artwork," "The Cyber-Head in the Shadow City," "The Ghosts That Haunt My Sleep in the Shadow City," "Higher Education in the Shadow City," "The History of the Shadow City," "The Iron Woman," "The Iron Woman Is Watching," "Mysteries of Light and Shade in the Shadow City," and "Rendezvous at a Café in the Shadow City,"

First Edition

ISBN 978-1-937128-40-1

Copyright © 2012
by Gary William Crawford and Bruce Boston

Photo Collage and Rendition:
Bruce Boston

Dark Regions Press
P.O. Box 1264
Colusa, CA 95932
www.darkregions.com

CONTENTS

Introduction
- 7   The Shadow City by Michael R. Collings

Texts
- 11   Welcome to the Shadow City
- 12   Shadow and Sun in the Shadow City
- 13   A Fine Education in the Shadow City
- 15   Higher Education in the Shadow City
- 17   A Sea of Shadow Umbrellas
- 19   A Night Storm in the Shadow City
- 20   The River Magnus Winds through the Shadow City
- 26   Poetry in the Shadow City
- 27   The Artwork
- 29   Insomnia
- 30   The History of the Shadow City
- 32   Lost in the Shadow City
- 33   The Web
- 34   Modern Medicine in the Shadow City
- 35   A Strange Disease
- 36   In Line at the Shadow City Pharmacy
- 38   Four Angles/Four Eyes
- 39   Reading Shadows
- 40   The Naming of Shadows in the Shadow City
- 41   Taking the Census in the Shadow City
- 42   The Shadow Thief
- 45   Kaleidoscope
- 46   Messengers from Hell
- 47   From the Shadow City Chamber of Commerce...
- 48   At the Shadow City Bus Depot
- 50   What the Traveler Saw
- 51   Never Take a Taxi in the Shadow City

53	I Met a Woman in the Shadow City
55	Dark Love in the Shadow City
57	The Intruder Has Stolen Nothing
59	Deadpan
60	Rebels in the Shadow City
63	Conflict in the Shadow City
64	Crucified in the Night of the Shadow City
67	They Put One Over
68	The Little God
69	Death and Ritual in the Shadow City
71	Last Things in the Shadow City
72	Mysteries of Light and Shade in the Shadow City
74	The Ghosts that Haunt My Sleep...
77	The Cyber-Head in the Shadow City
79	The Psychological Experiment Station
81	The Iron Woman
83	The Iron Woman Is Watching
85	The Final Word in the Shadow City
87	The Artistry of Punishment
92	The Knave of Shadows
93	Rendezvous at a Café in the Shadow City

Images

10	Skyscrapers in the Shadow City
21	Deserted Factories on the River Magnus
31	Father Mark
43	The Shadow Thief
49	Last Stop: The Shadow City
61	Rebels in the Shadow City
75	The Message in the Dots
95	The Iron Woman

The Shadow City

by Michael R. Collings

In this collaborative volume of poetry and images, Bruce Boston and Gary William Crawford seductively insinuate their readers into a City of Shadows....a city overhung with shadows, constructed from shadows, peopled by shadows. It is an eerie place, a mysterious and evil place.

Within the covers of this book, we meet a cast of fearsome characters: the ghosts of monks, who inculcate a brand of un-knowledge into their students; the Iron Woman, whose graduate studies include "chicanery, duplicity,/thievery, bribery, exculpation"; the Monitors of Mystery, police who see everything, hear everything, seem to be everywhere. First-person narrators remain largely undefined except for a single act or stance that separates them from the shadows, until they are absorbed again by the dark.

Even the landscape is inimical. The River Magnus is "deadly and capricious," sporting monstrous fish, lined with decaying remnants of buildings and empty lots clotted with rats and debris. The medical clinic deals in death-in-life, not life. Buses arrive in the Shadow City to deposit passengers. They never pick them up.

Worse yet for the denizens of this world — but notable for readers of this visionary dystopian collection — language itself is at times a pared-down shadow of traditional poetic diction, the underlying rhythm of lines and stanzas are present, but strangely muted. Imagery frequently fades into shadowy vagueness . . . intentionally, at times brilliantly so. Echoing the darkness of the words are intermittent images, black and white, umbral, at times chimerical, that resonate with the language to create fantastical depths.

To say that reading *Notes from the Shadow City* is a delight might be misleading; to say that it is unsettling, disconcerting, provocative, and remarkable is to scratch the surface of the shadows and begin to reveal the genius beneath.

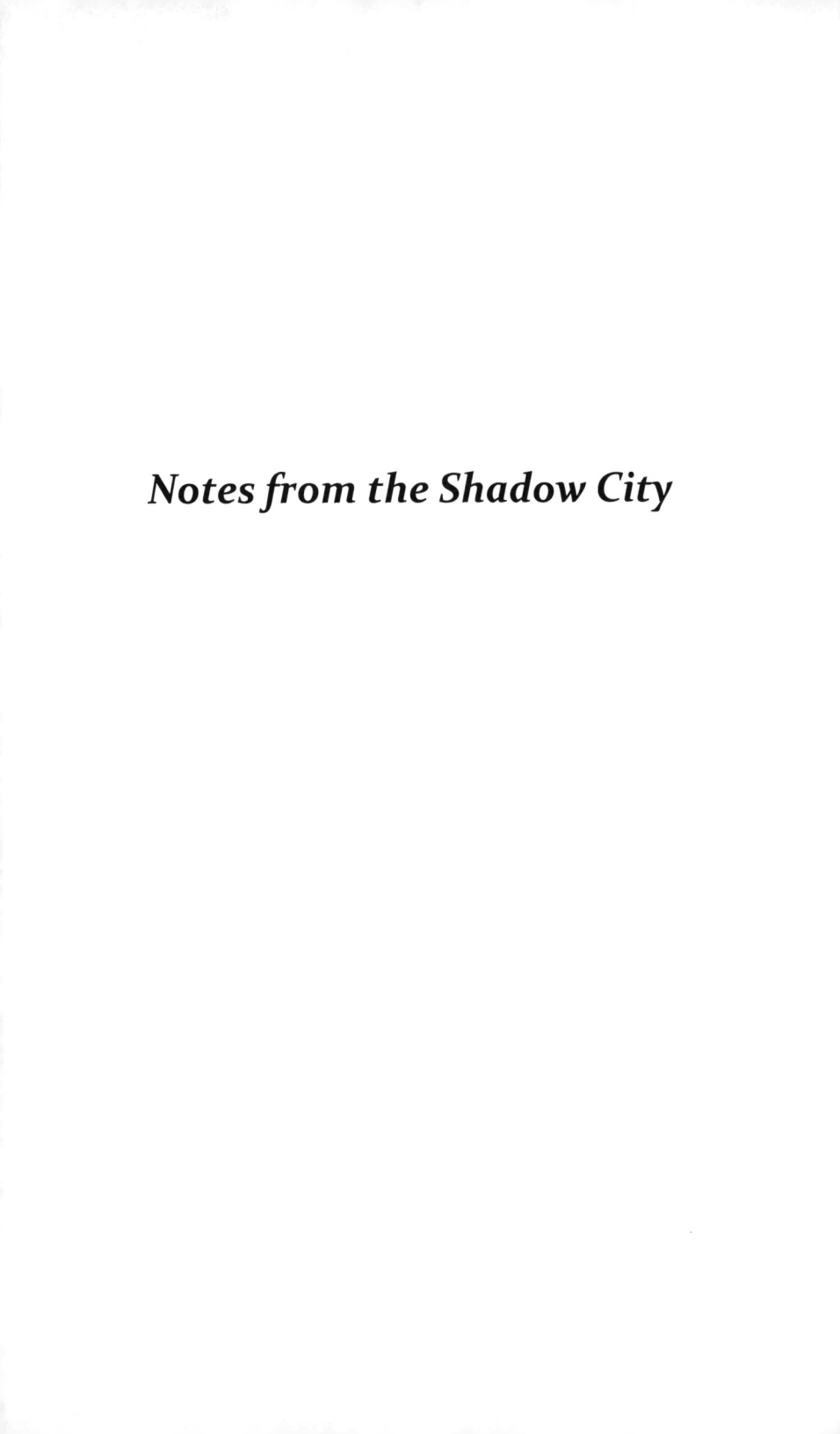

Notes from the Shadow City

Skyscrapers in the Shadow City

Welcome to the Shadow City
Gary William Crawford

Few have heard of the Shadow City.
Even fewer have been there.
Some say it existed thousands of years ago.
Some say it exists only in the future.
Others say it never existed at all.

It is both a legend and a dream.
And the words in their ancient tomes
are merely ghosts.
The core of this place is black:
It has a perverse propensity for evil.

So, for some the Shadow City
Is merely a slice of time
That cannot be entered or exited.
It is for no one or no thing.

Shadow and Sun in the Shadow City
Bruce Boston

Shadows in the Shadow City
cluster around us, umbras

and penumbras overlapping
in intricate complexity.

Shadows so thick we feel
the breath of their weight

like cloth on our backs.
Shadows so long and hallowed

they encompass time and space
in their lightless embrace.

When the sun appears in
the sliver of sky that rims

the buildings' highest floors
and strikes the street below,

blinding in its brightness,
rabid in its raw exposure,

responsible citizens scurry
for the cool random dark.

A Fine Education in the Shadow City
Crawford/Boston

All the children in the
Shadow City receive a fine
education cloaked in shadow

and tempered by betrayal.
Their teachers are the
ghosts of corrupt monks

who have been resurrected
from the unearthed past.
The children cannot grasp

the symbols and equations
that overflow the pages
of their books and writhe

over the walls and ceilings.
Sometimes the pages
are bound out of order

or inexplicably blank.
Still they learn what they
have been taught to learn

and they learn it by rote,
until its shadow litanies
are graven in their brains.

Each time the bell sounds,
electronic and insistent,
the children single-file

into the mirrored hallways,
where their lockers float
in a sea of misdirection.

No matter how many times
they change the combinations,
the ghost monks know them all.

Higher Education in the Shadow City
Boston/Crawford

They said knowledge was the key
to success in the Shadow City,
the right kind of knowledge.
The Iron Woman was in charge

of selecting all topics for study,
and she was perversely creative.
We studied chicanery, duplicity,
thievery, bribery, exculpation,

confession and redemption.
She would pace back and forth
in the front of the classroom,
instilling each lesson by rote.

We studied shadows and how
they can be slyly transformed
by the manipulation of light.
She held a stick that clicked

solidly on the chalkboard
or lashed out at her charges.
We watched shadows climb
like insects across the walls,

changing shapes as they went.
We suffered wild accusations
and committed to memory
the Liturgies of Father Mark.

For the final exam we picked
the name of a citizen at random
to confuse and persecute with
diverse bureaucratic errors,

to terrorize by phone calls
and with late-night searches
until they freely confessed
whatever crime we chose.

If we passed with honors
we were assured a sinecure
in the dark hierarchy
of the Shadow City.

A Sea of Shadow Umbrellas
Bruce Boston

There are no seasons
in the Shadow City.

Summer slips into fall
and the sky is a bit darker.

Winter slips into spring
and the sky grows brighter.

But as each year passes
there never seems to be

quite as much light
as there was before.

Rain falls in any season,
down from heavy clouds.

The streets are clogged
with shadow umbrellas

bobbing this way and that,
anonymous as the shadow

hands that hold them,
passing down the streets

in steady streams,
humpback beetles

intent on their purpose,
creatures of a hive mind,

wet black petals
floating on a shadow sea.

The Night Storm in the Shadow City
Gary William Crawford

The rain sounds like
the beating of wings.
The birds know the rain,
and I hear their fluttering
in my sleep.

This dream became a nightmare
about a storm in the Shadow City.
The wings of the venerable darkness
settle over the cold, lifeless skyscrapers
and the squalid streets below.

The people are starving here,
but what they hunger for is not food.

The men I lust after populate the bars,
and bait people like me, a homosexual
who has been beaten by these evil men,
the Monitors of Mystery.

I am afraid of their beauty
that draws me like a magnet,
and I die into them,
the wings of night
carrying me upward
above the storm.

The River Magnus Winds through the Shadow City
Bruce Boston

The River Magnus
winds through
the Shadow City
where songs are sung
with the tuneless solidity
of ancient cantos,
cancerous dirges
for a dirty river,
thick with the debris
of a failed population.

The dismal shores
of the River Magnus
are lined by fences
topped with barbwire,
by empty warehouses,
by deserted factories
surrounded by weeds,
their high patchworks
of broken windows
revealing nothing
but blackness beyond.

The dismal shores
of the River Magnus
are lined by scattered
and overgrown lots,
where rats and feral

Deserted Factories on the River Magnus

cats and other vermin
practice the survival
of the fittest, by the
unkempt backyards
of clapboard houses
sinking into desuetude,
the kind of houses
in which you imagine
a crazy old lady or
serial killer might live.

The River Magnus
is a deadly and
capricious river,
changing its course
with the rains,
which can rage
at any time of year,
pummeling down
from leaden clouds
in stinging icy droplets,
a smattering of hail,
or a torrential roar
that sweeps roads
and houses away,
so entire districts
once on land
lie underwater.

The River Magnus
is a deadly and
capricious river that

rampages beyond its
banks in any season,
sending out a net
of streaming tributaries,
smudge gray snakes
crawling beneath
a smudged sky.

When the rains subside
and the River Magnus
returns to its course,
flooded areas surface,
streets and buildings
coated with the river's
slime and sludge,
often stained by
a lime white fungus
that raises blisters
on the flesh of
all who touch it.

When the rains subside
and the River Magnus
returns to its course,
the areas flooded
are condemned
and cordoned off
as uninhabitable
for years at a time.

Only the starving
choose to fish

in the infected waters
of the River Magnus,
and their catches
are never the same,
except for being
goggled-eyed and
monstrous and
covered with
black sores,
evil mutations
of perverted genes,
reeking of chemicals
and human waste.

Only suicides
and mad fools
choose to swim
in the vile waters
of the River Magnus,
dank with the sheen
of oil and garbage,
and those that do
rarely return
to the shore,
even as corpses,
for something lives
in those evil currents,
a creature that devours
and excretes,
feeding off the city,
consuming its bile
and diverse refuse,

adding its own stench
to the riot of decay.

The River Magnus
winds through
the Shadow City
where songs are sung
with the tuneless solidity
of ancient cantos,
suicide songs sung
in a minor key,
murderous ones
in a major key,
mean litanies
one and all,
cancerous dirges
for a dirty river,
thick with the debris
of a failed population.

Poetry in the Shadow City
Gary William Crawford

The professors of literature
in the Shadow City
review every poem
for anything that goes against
their god.

A poet who wrote a sonnet cycle
about the evil of the place
wanted to publish it,
but the professors saw
that he must be condemned.

His punishment was harsh:
They cut off his hands
as they laughed at him
and called him a fool.

They made him swim
with no hands in the burning lake.
They would not let him die.

I think he still lives,
and they will not
let me see him.

I can only cry in rage and horror.
And I have the poems he wrote.

The Artwork
Gary William Crawford

I had training as an artist
in the Shadow City.
The only thing I could
draw or paint was an image
of the President holding
a rifle with the background
of a sunset.

I was taught to draw and
paint this image from
my earliest years.
I knew nothing else
about art.

I met a girl at the university
who was an artist too.
Like me all she could paint
was the image of the President
as I have described.

I fell in love with her,
and as I got to know her
I discovered that she
had drawn an image of me
holding a book.

I loved her even though
she had committed a heinous

crime. We were married
in the fall of the year
even though I knew she
was a sinner.

One autumn morning I got up
early to see the sunrise
and I painted it with no other
image. We were both criminals,
and one of my wife's friends
discovered the paintings
and reported us to the
Monitors of Mystery,
the wicked lawmen.

Now I know they are coming
for us to send us to prison
and I am plotting an escape.
May the forces of creation help us.

Insomnia
Gary William Crawford

Some people are insomniacs
in the Shadow City.
They walk the streets at all hours,
craving sleep and dreams,
but the Monitors of Mystery
distract them to keep them awake.

They say that dreaming gives
the citizens too much freedom.
In this place, as everywhere,
the deepest of dreams
are a necessity for wholeness.

But the lawmen and the high priests
squelch the healing that sleep offers.
So the people go through their lives
forever on the edge in a twilight world
of madness and death.

The History of the Shadow City
Bruce Boston

Father Mark orders me to construct a definitive history of the Shadow City, concise and precise, rich and informative. I summon what enthusiasm I can for the task, yet every other time I tap into the data cores for source material, the screen darkens as if a thick shadow or a gloved hand has passed across it. And once it clears again, the data I receive has changed from the time before. I no longer know what to believe.

As the deadline nears, I decide to fashion a history of the Shadow City from what little I know — or think I know — and once I have committed myself to the task, it all comes more easily than I could imagine. With names that never existed and precipitous events that never transpired, I fabricate a tale ripe for any newsstand or public broadcast, concise and precise, rich and informative.

Father Mark shakes his finger at me. "I'm afraid you have failed like the others. There is no valor in the history of the Shadow City, no earth-shaking deeds, no rewards for heroes, no pride. There is nothing for you to learn here but sacrifice and invalidation."

As I return to my cell, and the next aspirant is called forth to begin this unwanted and impossible task, the Shadow City remains without a history anyone would want to believe.

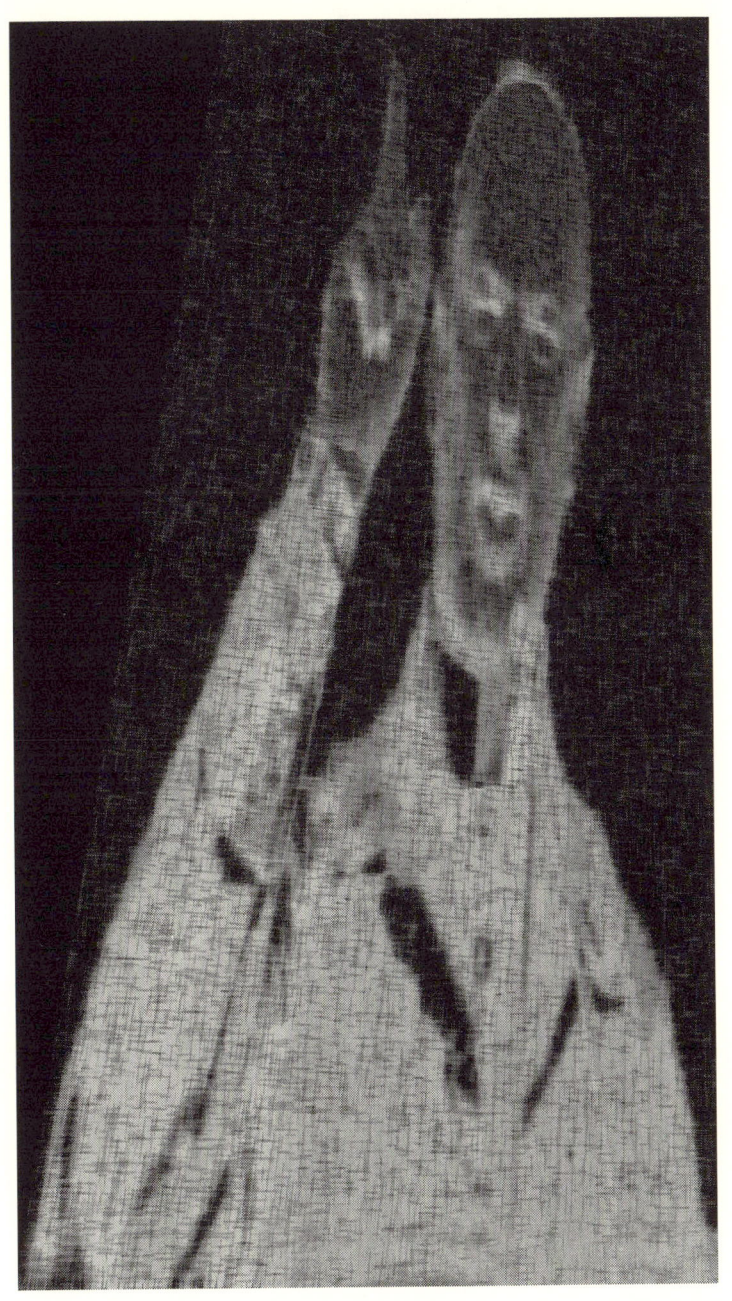

Father Mark

Lost in the Shadow City
Bruce Boston

Lost voices in the Shadow City
cry out against the dark
yet never expect
to be heard.

Lost arms in the Shadow City
reach out to embrace
something substantial
that has survived.

Lost eyes in the Shadow City
strain to see the random
strands of light that
penetrate the gloom.

Lost thoughts in the Shadow City
live with the dying hope
they could encounter
a kindred mind.

Lost souls in the Shadow City
wander the noir streets
of shade upon shade
only half alive.

The Web
Crawford/Boston

Illness is a part of daily existence
in the Shadow City.
In the pockets of this disease,
soul-eating bacteria thrive.

I, the prophet of the city,
am not immune to its
feverish infections.
Each day I humiliate myself
and bring forth phantoms
that reduce me to
no more than a spider,
spinning the web of sickness
in the darkest corners of the city.

I cry out in agony,
but continue to move eight-legged
from shadow to shadow,
my jaundiced eyes
glimmering in the dark.

I am doomed to perpetually
create this web of affliction,
a morbid pathology
of my disintegrating self.

Modern Medicine in the Shadow City
Gary William Crawford

This is a medical clinic in the Shadow City:

The nurses wear black with high-heeled
shoes that click down the black marble
hallways of each private hell.
They sell themselves to the patients.
The patients like that because
they think the pleasures the nurses offer heal.
They induce a slow, yet powerful
orgasmic feeling to the average man
on the street who walks down the sidewalk
hungering for release.

The doctor stands at a pulpit, screaming.
He beats a bible
that is an encyclopedia of illusion
that eventually numbs and kills.

In this way the doctors and the nurses
immunize themselves against the truth
with lies that are like the drugs
they administer, only placebos
to retard the inevitability of death.

A Strange Disease
Gary William Crawford

It is a strange disease
that afflicts some in the Shadow City.
The symptoms appear to be
a madness, but they are not.

The afflicted indulge in a ritual
that goes unknown
except to the initiated.
These are the mystics
of the Shadow City.

They make me their sacrifice:
binding me in chains,
they force me onto a pyre,
In moments I am burning.
They dance around me chanting
and feeding the fire.

In my death, they don't know
I am set free to be the mystic
of all mystics, to carry the disease
through the infinite.

In Line at the Shadow City Pharmacy
Bruce Boston

Shadows wait in line
at the Shadow City Pharmacy.

Some are bent with age.
They inch forward
on shadow walkers.
Others are obese,
their shadows blooming
like rain-swollen clouds.
Or they are terribly frail,
their shadows like sticks
that jerk and twitch.

Some look healthy
enough yet they find
themselves trapped
in line with other
shadows nonetheless.

They all seek specific
medications for very
specific ailments,
salves and potions,
and soporifics.

They seek cure-alls
and temporary relief,
and most of all pills
secured in cloudy
plastic amber vials.

The shadow priest
behind the counter
takes his own time
filling and dispensing
each sacred prescription.

He is a precise man
who seldom speaks,
a perpetual frown
etched on his narrow
features beneath
gold-rimmed glasses
and colorless eyes.

And his shadow
in the fluorescent light
is sharply etched
as a surgeon's knife
as it strikes the tall
shelves behind him
and the scarred
linoleum of the floor.

The line of ailing
mendicants grows
longer and longer
as time dissolves
in life-lost minutes
in the shadow of night.

Four Angles/Four Eyes
Gary William Crawford

They are taking my picture
from four angles.
They are the Monitors of Mystery,
the wicked lawmen
in the Shadow City.

I pick at the scab
of my madness
until it bleeds again.
I have harmed no one.
Yet they call me on the phone,
speaking in a coded language.

They take me to a hospital
in the garbage dump
outside the city.
"This is the proper place for you,"
say the Monitors of Mystery.
Every day they take
my picture from four angles.

I forever read with four eyes
a passage in one of their horrible bibles,
and await the darkness.

Reading Shadows
Gary William Crawford

Reading is difficult in the Shadow City
because the wicked lawmen
— those Monitors of Mystery —
make sure that readers can't concentrate.
Reading is undesirable because
the people would think too much
and see the evil everywhere.

A place of no libraries or bookstores,
it has brainwashing as part
of the school curriculum.
It's all for their own good.

But I, a young, frightened student,
discovered that I could read shadows.
I began to question what they taught me.
My gift of reading shadows
allowed my brain to be clear.

Liberated, I managed to find others
who could read shadows,
and we formed our own school
that gave us a way out.
In finding others we were free.

The Naming of Shadows in the Shadow City
Bruce Boston

Intense

One of the darkest shadows
in any gathering of shadows.
Resides in the deepest
shade of the umbra.

Weak

A background shadow
that seldom receives
more than the barest
shadow of a glance.

Variable

Wanders from the umbra
to the penumbra
in no sensible fashion.
To be used
but not trusted

Invisible

The shadow that
cloaks all other shadows
in the Shadow City.

Taking the Census in the Shadow City
Gary William Crawford

The Monitors of Mystery
are taking the census here.
All the names are different,
but they are all
the same dark shadows.

You cannot distinguish your shadow
in the Shadow City
because it has
so many companions.
You are utterly alone
in the crowd,
and thus oppressed
by the powers of horror.

The Shadow Thief
Bruce Boston

The shadow thief
yanks you into an alley,
presses a knife
against your throat,
and demands you empty
your pockets completely.
He picks and chooses
at his pleasure.

The shadow thief takes
the watch from your wrist
and places it on his own,
pausing to admire
it for a moment
in ritual satisfaction.

The shadow thief
materializes a syringe
from his shabby overcoat
or shiny leather jacket.
By a swift jab of the spike
he anesthetizes you
instantaneously.

With that selfsame knife,
sharp and unclean,
in that selfsame alley,
dark and unclean,

The Shadow Thief

the shadow thief
skillfully extricates
one of your organs
for sale on the black market.

The shadow thief
yanks you into an alley,
presses a knife
against your throat,
and demands you empty
your pockets completely.
He picks and chooses
at his pleasure.

He excavates the sum
of your hidden fears.

The shadow thief
has no need for your soul,
with that he will leave you,
naked and shivering,
bloody and violated,
in the long night
shadows of the city.

Kaleidoscope
Gary William Crawford

His life was ever changing,
like the nightmarish places
in the Shadow City,
and he wore dark glasses
and saw things as in a kaleidoscope.
He went from every day, hour,
and moment to moment,
feeling he had lost himself,
changing over and over again.

He walked the streets, that were
illuminated by the fires of hell.
The ever-changing flames,
like the hypnotic kaleidoscope,
drove him to madness.
The wizard he feared all his life
told him to destroy himself.

He was my friend,
but the good I saw in him
was not enough to keep him alive.
I found him dead in an alleyway
in the seediest part
of the Shadow City,
his eyes open and flashing
like a neon sign.
His death was his final metamorphosis.

Messengers from Hell
Gary William Crawford

In my attic room
in the Shadow City
they are sending me
messengers from their hell.
They inflame my mind
and set my eyes on fire.

The place is burning,
but the firemen
only fuel the flames.
I'm afraid I will die
if I go to the doctors
because they are in collusion
with the police.

They are coming for me
to lynch me so I can live
frozen in time
and haunt the haunters,
these ghosts that are alive.

**Quotes from the Shadow City
Chamber of Commerce Brochure**
Bruce Boston

"Welcome to the Shadow City,
where you can leave your self behind."

"Give us your shadow
and we'll soon give you ten thousand more."

"The way we see it, the thicker and darker
the shadows — the richer the shadows."

"You don't really need to see much
more than a shadow to get by."

"Don't believe what you've heard.
Some of us are almost solid."

"No need to bring the sunscreen!"

"Not responsible for lost identities."

At the Shadow City Bus Depot
Bruce Boston

The thinnest and frailest shadows in the Shadow City are those of the weak, the old, the disenfranchised.

Such as those one can find on any evening inhabiting the long wooden benches that divide the rectangular waiting room of the Shadow City Bus Depot. They are not waiting for a bus, or anything else for that matter, except in their dreams. They are seeking temporary shelter from the elements and the gangs that roam the night town streets of the Shadow City.

Their bare shadows leave the slightest stain upon the highly polished wood of the benches. Yet the Shadow City does not concert stains.

The miscreants are rousted from their infestation by shadows far more substantial than their own. They are driven beyond the swinging double doors and into the night, where they will remain invisible.

Soon the doors are motionless again. The room is empty. The polished wood of the benches shines only for itself.

No one is waiting for a bus. The buses that stop here leave passengers off. They never pick them up.

Last Stop: The Shadow City

What the Traveler Saw
Gary William Crawford

The traveler to the Shadow City
approaches its outskirts
by way of a road to nowhere.
An artist himself,
he looks at this place
through the eyes
of the porcelains,
the ancient artifacts regarded
as unholy by the citizens.

The visitor is horrified
by what he sees:
the people wear dark glasses
at midnight and pray
to no gods except the ones
of pure sensation.

The traveler is saddened
by this place where the truth
is buried, like the artifacts,
with the old gods,
who will never be resurrected.

Never Take a Taxi in the Shadow City
Bruce Boston

There are no yellow
or checkered cabs here.
Only the dull matte gray
of government vehicles for hire.

And atop the roof of each,
a spike of white light
with the word "Taxi" falling
in a pyramid so that each letter
is wider than the one before.

Those spikes emit a light
that illuminates its singular
message but nothing more.
It is a light that casts no light
or shadow beyond itself.

Even the roof of the vehicle
that carries it remains invisible
in the enduring and impenetrable
night of the Shadow City.

And night is the only time
these taxis can be found
roaming the leaden streets
in search of patrons and prey.

Such vehicles are often driven
by strangers to the Shadow City.
They speak with accents when
they bother to speak at all.
They were not born in the
Shadow City but sent here
by some calamity or chance.

Or merely found their way
here running from the light.
Sometimes you wonder if
these may be the only true
denizens of the Shadow City.

That while you were shaving
or working or traveling below
ground in the tunnel trains,
this has become their world
more than it is yours.

From your brief and unintelligible
interchange when you entered
the narrow confines of the vehicle,
you cannot be sure the driver has
understood where you want
to go or a thing you've said.

As he carries you on into
a night you fail to recognize.

I Met a Woman in the Shadow City
Bruce Boston

I met a woman at the airport bar in the Shadow City.

Planes rarely land or take off at the Shadow City Airport anymore. Still we congregate in its decaying rooms and stroll its shabby walkways as if they did. Pretending we are about to jet off for a weekend to Denver or Jakarta or some other fabled land we are never to visit in the flesh, we strike up conversations with complete strangers.

I met a woman at the airport bar in the Shadow City. The room was veiled in smoke and she was cloaked in shadow. Fog swirled across the tarmac beyond the tinted windows. Runway lights shone so faintly in the distance one could not be sure they were there at all.

We shared a bottle of wine, a mature Cabernet, in the bar of the Shadow City Airport. It was an expensive wine, rich and ruby red, worth every drop. Smooth and full-bodied from the first swallow. The label claimed blackberries and cherries, but I tasted mainly plums. Perhaps a hint of cherry in the bouquet.

I met a woman at the airport bar in the Shadow City. She frowned every time she took a sip. Or at least what I took to be a frown beyond the smoke, beyond her shadow in the airport bar of the Shadow City.

She was a petite blonde, no more than twenty-five, a handsome and large-boned redhead, thirty-six, a sultry brunette, dark of complexion, eighteen going on forty. A shadow can be anything you want it to be at the airport bar in the Shadow City.

We spoke of the discomforts of flying and how they had grown worse over the years. She hinted at her own jaded history, hard days on the road and rocky ones in harness. She said she was a stranger in the Shadow City, only waiting for a connecting flight. Though she would never mention her destination.

That was how I knew her for what she was, one of those ghost shadows who roam the decaying chambers and shabby corridors of the Shadow City Airport, those who are lost in transit, who have left one world behind and will never arrive at another.

When I suggested a second bottle, she turned away. And then she turned back.

She looked at me through the veil of smoke and told me I was only a shadow and not really traveling anywhere. She said she had known my kind before, too many times, and that I did not belong here.

She left the airport bar in the Shadow City quickly. Almost at a run. She was already late for a flight that would not arrive. Within seconds, it seemed as if she had never been there at all.

The only evidence of her passage was half a glass of wine she had left on the table. It was an expensive wine, well worth savoring.

I decided not to drink it.

Dark Love in the Shadow City
Gary William Crawford

He came to me,
at first, imperceptibly,
then more vividly
through the labyrinths
beneath the Shadow City.
I heard his deep voice
wrap around me,
almost stroking me,
echoing through the place
and sending me to a lake
at the city's core
from which millions of ants
emerged to tear my skin.

His voice grew louder
as I was eaten, my blood
oozing out of my pores
into the boiling lake
at the base of the volcano
above the city.

I was finally devoured,
all the while hearing
his obscenities that enhanced
the vicious torture I would feel
at his hands.

Was he not in his way
giving me his love,
a love that drew me deeper
into his spell?
I could feel his body against mine,
sending me into an orgasm
as my blood flowed into rivulets.

I will find no peace here:
his sexuality was of a kind
I had never known.
I died at that moment,
as the Monitors of Mystery,
the evil lawmen,
cut off my head
and gave my body parts to him.

My inmost self
was the source of his pleasure,
and that moment of ecstasy
is, like the city,
frozen in time.

The Intruder Has Stolen Nothing
Gary William Crawford

Someone has been leaving me notes
in my attic room in the Shadow City.
Each day I find a new note.
The symbols on them
crawl, like bacteria, on the floor,
then take flight and spread
to the walls, but are unintelligible.
How did the intruder get in?
The doors were locked.

I had a dream last night
of a small door in a closet
that was an escape
from the horrible place.
If I didn't have dreams,
I couldn't go on.

The intruder has fueled my dreams,
so in breaking and entering,
he leaves me a gift
And there is no need
To call the wicked lawmen,
The Monitors of Mystery.

I sit in a corner,
talking nonsense,
and in this madness,

I leave my own notes
to this messenger of dreams,
this angel-prowler,
and beat him at his own game.

Deadpan
Gary William Crawford

You looked at me strangely:
a deadpan for a dead man.
As the days passed in the Shadow City:
another look from one of your friends
that reflected your look.
Then a few days later:
another look from another
of your friends
that mirrored the previous one.

Yet another look
from another friend
that mirrored the first.
Then one night:
a look from another
of your friends
through my bedroom window.

Why is it that there are
some changes in my body,
terrible changes,
as I look in my bedroom mirror
and see you staring back?

Rebels in the Shadow City
Bruce Boston

They publish incendiary
tracts filled with lies
and vile accusations.

Some see them
as saints and saviors
and righteous rebels.

Some say they are
only hooligans
and vicious miscreants.

You can find them
in the Shadow City
each and every night,

lurking in causeways,
lounging negligent
by taverns and pool halls,

awaiting an honest citizen
on a late night errand
or sleepless walk.

They claim to
steal from the rich
and give to the poor,

yet their hidden coffers
are no doubt heavy
with their own spoils.

Rebels in the Shadow City

And when we attempt
to apprehend them
we discover that

their shadows ripple
and flicker with no
discernible pattern.

They flee incessantly
from one transient
safe house to another.

Yet a day of reckoning
will arrive when the
truth shall be revealed.

Thieves or rebels,
their bodies will bleed
without redemption

in the chambers
and candlelit dungeons
of immaculate priests,

where the torturer
practices and perfects
his singular occupation,

and there is no question
that cannot be answered
with sufficient pain.

Conflict in the Shadow City
Gary William Crawford

They are called to war,
but I tell them they are wrong to kill.
The army officers give me drugs
to shut me up.
They lock me away
in one of their padded cells.
Here I am a visionary who sees
the soldiers, one by one,
disappear by means of trapdoors
in the theater of war
and fall into another dimension.

I give them peace here,
and they wonder why
they didn't know this before.
I free them from the Shadow City,
and they forever dream.

Crucified in the Night of the Shadow City
Bruce Boston

You sense that someone
or something is following you,
so your footfalls hasten
down the branching
and intersecting streets
of the Shadow City,
and in your haste
you are soon lost
in a twisting maze
of crooked thoroughfares
and tortuous byways.

And as you hurry on
the cityscape that
surrounds you changes
from government domes
to dark skyscrapers,
their facades monolithic,
sheer and indifferent,
to tightly shuttered
department stores,
to dim cafeterias
emitting the stench
of grease and smoke,
to bars and drifters
and corner hustlers
and fallen storefronts,
their windows soaped
or boarded over,
to darker streets still,

inhabited by derelicts,
whose skeleton hands
reach for spare change,
whose voices assault
you in a ragged chorus
of pleas both piteous
and intimidating.

And as you hurry on
your world seems
increasingly steeped
in a thick fluidity
of blurred shadows,
for here there are
no street lights,
no street signs,
no signs of life
of any kind
but for your own
faltering steps
and the dogged
presence behind
that you sense
but cannot see.

Your flight ends
in the cul-de-sac
of a dank alley,
a chain-link fence
barring your passage.
You press your
hands and body

against the cold
metal of the links
as if you could
pass through
and escape farther
into the darkness.

Odd noises emanate
from beyond the fence,
and all at once there
is a spotlight flare of
blinding illumination.

You find yourself
crucified in silhouette
by your own shadow
stretched across the
worn and littered
asphalt of the alley.

And at the mouth
of the alleyway,
beyond your shadow,
just beyond that
stark perimeter
of falling light,
the stray beasts
of night come
slouching toward you
ready to feed.

They Put One Over
Gary William Crawford

There is an emptiness in the Shadow City.
In the hearts and minds of its citizens,
there is mourning for their god's passing.
The people line the streets,
hoping to get a glimpse of the corpse
as the funeral procession passes.

First come musicians playing maddening music
that only sounds like noise.
Following are the Monitors of Mystery,
the wicked lawmen.
Then there are the high priests,
who praise the dead god.

His flesh has dropped away,
And his skeleton is made of gold.
What has been kept from the people
Is that their god died thousands of years ago.
This elaborate hoax, engineered by the priests,
Is the greatest mystery of the Shadow City,
the very greatest lie for which they pray.

Father Mark smiles
as the women and children cry.
The clerics know the truth,
And a deep, cold darkness that
Can never be erased falls
On the inhabitants,
And they worship
No one and no thing at all.

The Little God
Gary William Crawford

They are trying to laugh
because it screams.
They can't be sure what it is:
mineral, vegetable, bird, ape?
But they know that it knows them,
and they are afraid.

Here in the Shadow City,
the citizens fear this god
because it tells them
the truth about themselves.
They desperately try
to prevent the bleeding that
the revelation causes.
They cling to their lives
and build churches that are
nothing more than circus sideshows.

In this way they immunize
themselves from the disease
in their blood they inherited
from the ancient past.
They desperately try
to stave off the blackness
and pray to the inexorable.

Death and Ritual in the Shadow City
Boston/Crawford

Death is rarely kind,
and less so in the Shadow City.

The priests of the Shadow City
have concocted a ceremony
that must be obeyed
with eidetic certainty.

Black limousines
carry the dearly departed
from the ghastly strains
of funeral parlors
to their earthy rewards.

The cemetery stands
stark and silent
in the dripping rain.

Dark figures gather
loosely round the open
pit of the grave
while the mimetic
words are mouthed.

An eavesdropper watches
from three trees away,
a priest in disguise,
to confirm that

the shadow gods
have been praised.

There,
the frozen scenario
is almost chiaroscuro
in its stark indelibility.

Then,
the first spade of dirt,
seeming more oily than wet,
strikes the polished wood.

Often it is the sickening
thud of that sound
that haunts one's mind
for years to come.

The priests make sure
it all goes like a clock
tolling the knells of Death,
a ceremonial apparition
to plague the living.

Death is rarely kind
and less so in the Shadow City.

He waits in the shadows
and then steps into the light,
Ritual like a fawning lover
on his arm.

Last Things in the Shadow City
Gary William Crawford

Some of the numbers and letters
are transposed or erroneous
in the bibles of the Shadow City.
I know it all means something,
something about me.

This is the world of illusion,
of imperfections and an obsession
with them: they tell me I am mad.
But I know that they are instead
playing tricks on me.
Their bibles forever test me
in some way to find the truth
in the last things.

Time vanishes in the Shadow City,
and in this hole in space
I am their prophet
in a padded cell,
where I write my own bibles
of a god that is no god,
and a life that is a death,
and a death that is a life.

Mysteries of Light and Shade in the Shadow City
Crawford/Boston

Some shadows have
no visible source.
They climb up steps
and clamber over walls,
they ripple down
crowded boulevards.

On residential byways.
they merge with
the deeper shadows
of trees and bushes.

These are shadows cast
by no visible objects,
they are shadows
without a maker.

I have seen a shadow
orchestra with shadow
couples dancing
to a ghostly pavane.
The music is real
but the players and
instruments are not.

I have seen shadows
gather in empty lots,
waiting to pounce

upon unwary citizens
and smother them
in cloaks of shade.

I scream in anger because
this place will kill me.
For I have discovered
that in the scattered
stains of illumination
that mar the darkness
of the Shadow City,
I have no shadow at all.

The Ghosts that Haunt My Sleep in the Shadow City
Boston/Crawford

There is only one television station in the Shadow City and it plays on all the channels. An endless round of shows exhibiting a deadening similarity: game shows, talent shows, stark morality plays affirming life in the Shadow City and how much worse it could be for all of us. And then there is the news, anchored by a priest or Monitor or one of their minions. Sometimes I pretend not to believe the news, but it is the only news I have.

Yet beyond these images that flit across the screen like dreams not of my making, I sense a more subtle and insidious form of mind control. Hidden in those repetitive images there are other images and another message.

On some nights when it is late and all the channels have signed off and I feel too tired to rise and get to bed, I watch those dots in their interminable and frenzied dance upon the screen. And after I stare long enough I can sense words flickering past too fast for my mind to comprehend or remember. Yet I know they are there and I know they are telling me something.

And I believe they must remain there during the shows, too. They are just more thoroughly hidden by a surface image. For what are the shows on the screen but a constant stream of ever changing dots?

Everybody must see the hidden words as I do. They know they are there, but they won't admit it. It's a secret that everyone has agreed upon.

Now I feel those same images like ghosts in my dreams,

The Message in the Dots

even the dreams I can't remember. And sometimes they haunt me in my waking hours, hovering like specters at the edge of consciousness, just beyond understanding.

I've been trying to watch less television because I'm sick of their lies. And I never watch the dots anymore at all. It would be easier if I had something to read. Or anything else to do. But I'm trying hard as I can.

For when I understand that message and those ghost images become my dreams and my life, I know I will be lost as the others.

The Cyber-Head in the Shadow City
Gary William Crawford

He likes to have his act together,
but the shadows betray him.
He is a weaver of magic symbols
that haunt the web and infiltrate,
like a political spy, the digital
vision of the people of the Shadow City.
He can sway the numbers of the blind
voters who place faith in his technology,
which he has embraced, vampiric,
like a lover, like a devil, to create
illusions of peace and contentment
with the people's world. Oh, yes,
with him all is well, but the Monitors
of Mystery, those wicked lawmen,
have his passwords, and they take
over the wicked programs he uses
to their advantage.

Lest he talk, he must be squelched.
The psychologists of the place
have designed a new website
that he can search — with colors,
signs, landscapes, all culminating
in a blue glow that is better than any
drug he has tried. They have him smiling.

The monitors have him on all
the screens with a grin so impressive

and fascinating that the people
watch him, awed, night and day.
He has their vote.

The Psychological Experiment Station
Gary William Crawford

There are rats everywhere.
I am trapped in this psychological
experiment station in the Shadow City
where there are no doors or windows
and nothing to eat but the rats.

The station is one of the more
hellish places in the city.
They try to squelch
any behavior that subverts
the powers of the leaders
and high priests.
The building is a perfect
rectangular box that has
only one entrance or exit,
and out of that door come
the newly transformed people,
but they say not everyone survives.

The evil psychiatrists in the Shadow City
are in collusion with the Monitors of Mystery,
those wicked lawmen, to make me their subject
and clock my horror in the hidden cameras
that penetrate the walls. They know I hate them,
but that is what they want. I scream,
cursing them to the most reverent hell.

I see the rats looking at me
with their red eyes,
waiting to slowly nibble me
away with their tiny teeth,

In time I become so hungry
that I decide to eat one of them.
Only to discover they are
impossible to catch.

The Iron Woman
Gary William Crawford

I always knew she was evil.
She had established herself
a place in Shadow City politics.
She was, as they say, "a pillar"
of the sick church that held
sway over the innocent and
ignorant citizens. They didn't know
what they were worshipping.

She was in collusion
with the high priests
and the wicked lawmen.
She also maintained a
position on the school board,
reviewing with the priests
and the professors at the
university what was taught
by the teachers,
who were required
to go through brainwashing
as part of their training.

I was a member of a secret
group of dissidents who believed
in love, but soon one spy member
infiltrated the group.
With her he set up a day and time for their
massacre, and I managed to

find a hiding place.
Now I write poetry furiously
in hopes that it will save me.

The Iron Woman Is Watching
Bruce Boston

She fills your dreams
with indelible reasons
for the exaltation
of mediocrity.

*The iron woman is
always watching you
in the Shadow City.*

Her vile tattoos
infest the slate
of your mind
like insects forged
in intimate enclaves
of pathology.

*The iron woman
is always watching
and judging you
in the Shadow City.*

She rakes your days
with hypotheses
brute and demanding
as the bits used
to tame wild horses.

*The iron woman is
always watching
and judging and
condemning you
in the Shadow City.*

Her spider song
is resplendent with sin,
with verses sharp
as a butcher's knife,
and a chorus
you know by heart.

*The iron woman
is always watching
and judging and
condemning you
to remain forever
in the Shadow City.*

The Final Word in the Shadow City
Bruce Boston

Words are destroyed
in the Shadow City
one by one and
in batches at a time.
Words vanish into
cracks and crevices
darker than our lives,
their definitions
expunged forever.

Books become
unreadable as the
parallel black bars
of the inspector's
stamp eradicate
entire passages.

Songs are unsingable
when their lyrics
are slashed and
there is no longer
any sense of rhyme.

As the shadows
quicken in layer
upon layer, erasing
the shades of our
language, stripping

away all subtlety
from our minds,
our thoughts slow
and thicken in kind.

Soon all that will
remain for us to
speak, to perceive,
to ponder, will be
a single word bound
by a singular intent
that comprises the
bereft vocabulary
of our lives.

The Artistry of Punishment
Gary William Crawford

The judge of the Shadow City
listens to the young man's
plea for freedom.
If freedom ever existed,
he hopes for it,
but feels he is lost in a maze
while the judge laughs at him.
The judge is known across the Shadow City
as being harsh and unyielding.
The young man's body quivers,
but he knows his crime is not that great.

The judge's sentence is creative
in its cruelty: the young man is told
he must suffer ten waking nightmares.

ONE

He is a child again
in a world of love and hope;
but he finds himself
lost in a thick wood
outside the Shadow City.
He can't be sure, but a brown
bear appears in the brush,
and its face resembles
that of his dead father.

TWO

At the funeral of a young girl
whom he loves as children love,
her eyes flutter open, and he cries
because he doesn't understand
how she can live again.

THREE

A boyhood friend dies
of what seems anemia.
The friend taps
on the young boy's window, asking,
"May I have some of your blood?
I'm so cold. I need your warm blood."

FOUR

He wakes one morning, feverish and cold,
and hungry for blood.
His mother takes him to a priest
in the Shadow City
who orders that a hot branding iron
be placed on the bites on his neck
and holy water be doused on the wounds.

FIVE

He is once again five years old,
and his pet cocker spaniel, Buff,

nuzzles him. The boy laughs
and pets his dog, but then,
Buff growls deeply
and bites him on his hand.

SIX

He is once again in second grade,
and the teacher
on whom he has a crush,
Mrs. McBride, announces
that her husband is a demon.
Turned against all males,
she pulls out a knife
and calls the boy's name.

SEVEN

He is in his teens,
and he is dating a young girl,
but to his horror,
he learns she is a witch.
He takes her to a drive-in movie,
and she performs strange incantations.
The characters in the movie step down
from the screen to talk to him.

EIGHT

He takes a job in a coffin factory;
and when he delivers coffins

to a funeral home,
he notices how deathly
pallid are the undertakers.
They smile, showing their
fangs, and one says,
"We've come to take you with us."

NINE

He marries a beautiful girl,
and on their wedding night,
he realizes that her father is
Lovecraft's character Wilbur Whateley.
When she takes off her clothes
he sees her skin is leathery
with numerous pulsating suckers,
like the tentacles of an octopus.

TEN

The child he fathers with his wife
is not of this world.
So ashamed and horrified,
he takes the child to a secluded wood,
kills the baby,
then kills himself.

CODA

The judge reads in the newspaper
of the young man's homicide and suicide,

but feels no remorse.
He was only doing his job.
He considers himself
a talented artist.

The Knave of Shadows
Bruce Boston

When I leave the Shadow City
it will be in the heat of day
and the blaze of a high noon sun.
The King of Shadows along
with his shady retinue
will have vanished
in the brightness.

When I leave the Shadow City
it will be swiftly
in the pitch of a night
overcast and moonless.
The Queen of Shadows
will be invisible
in the blanket dark.

When I leave the Shadow City
the Knave of Shadows
will trail behind me,
stretching back for miles
beneath the sunset sky,
thinner and thinner
yet never severed,
stretching back to a world
I once inhabited.

Rendezvous at a Café in the Shadow City
Bruce Boston

They were always punctual. They arrived at the entrance at the same moment and greeted one another formally. He bowed slightly and she nodded her head in return. He opened the door for her and slipped in behind, quickly following her clicking heels to a booth at the rear of the room.

It wasn't until they were seated opposite one another with the curtain drawn that they relaxed and smiled openly. Although there were no laws prohibiting it, they preferred not to be seen together. That was why they often chose an out-of-the-way café on a street cloaked more thoroughly in shadow than most.

They were not clandestine lovers, though on occasion they had slept together, made what could be called a kind of love. Rather they were political strategists of the ever changing malfeasance of the Shadow City.

They were not even friends, not in the normal sense of the word. Rather they were allies, conspirators in ongoing machinations to enhance their power and gain further wealth in the Shadow City.

She removed her long leather gloves, revealing long pale hands that looked naked without them. "I have much to tell you," she informed him.

"And I, you," he answered in kind. "We have a great deal to discuss." He leaned forward, resting the black sleeves of his cassock on the table, clasping his palms together with fingers intertwined.

A waiter poked his head through the curtain to take their orders. The Iron Woman requested a chef's salad and a glass of sparkling Chardonnay. Father Mark opted for a stout malt liquor, room temperature, and the grilled and blackened plaice.

Through a lengthy and intense repartee — the waiter returning over and again to fill their glasses — they discussed what shadows had outlived their usefulness, what shadows needed to be advanced as pawns in their game. They plotted with a cold and vicious joy how to make the world of the Shadow City even darker than it was.

The Iron Woman

Gary William Crawford is a scholar, poet, and short story writer. He is the author of books such as *Ramsey Campbell* and *Robert Aickman: An Introduction*. In 1979 he founded Gothic Press, which published the journal *Gothic* and now publishes the free online journal *Le Fanu Studies*. His poetry collections *The Shadow City* and *The Phantom World* were both Bram Stoker Award Finalists. His short-story collections are *Gothic Fevers* and *Mysteries of Von Domarus*. He co-edited *Reflections in a Glass Darkly: Essays on J. Sheridan Le Fanu*, and with Brian J. Showers compiled *Joseph Sheridan Le Fanu: A Concise Bibliography*. He lives in Baton Rouge, Louisiana. www.gwcgothicpress.com

Bruce Boston lives in Ocala, Florida, once known as the City of Trees, with his wife, writer-artist Marge Simon, and the ghosts of two cats. He is the author of fifty books and chapbooks, including the novels *The Guardener's Tale* and *Stained Glass Rain*. His poetry and fiction have appeared in hundreds of publications, including *Asimov's Science Fiction, Amazing Stories, Weird Tales, Strange Horizons, Realms of Fantasy, Year's Best Fantasy and Horror*, and *The Nebula Awards Showcase*. One of the leading genre poets for more than a quarter century, Boston has won the Bram Stoker Award for Poetry, the *Asimov's* Readers Award, and the Rhysling Award for Speculative Poetry, each a record number of times. He has also received a Pushcart Prize for Fiction and the Grandmaster Award of the Science Fiction Poetry Association. www.bruceboston.com

Michael R. Collings, a former professor of creative writing and literature at Pepperdine University, has published numerous critical works, collections of poetry (including *The Nephiad: An Epic Poem in XII Books*), and the novels *The Slab* and *The House beyond the Hill*. Visit his website at www.starshineandshadows.com/.